Mighty Mizzling Mouse

Mighty Mizzling Mouse

FRISO HENSTRA

J.B. Lippincott / New York

Library of Congress Cataloging in Publication Data
Henstra, Friso.
    Mighty mizzling mouse.

    Summary: Wordless story about a wild cat-mouse chase.
    [1. Stories without words.   2. Mice—Fiction.
3. Cats—Fiction]   I. Title.
PZ7.H3987Mi 1983   [E]   82-48459
ISBN 0-397-32003-5
ISBN 0-397-32004-3 (lib. bdg.)

1   2   3   4   5   6   7   8   9   10
First Edition

"To my granddaughter Maaike"